Usborne

Poppy and Sam's
Complete Book
of
Farmyard Tales

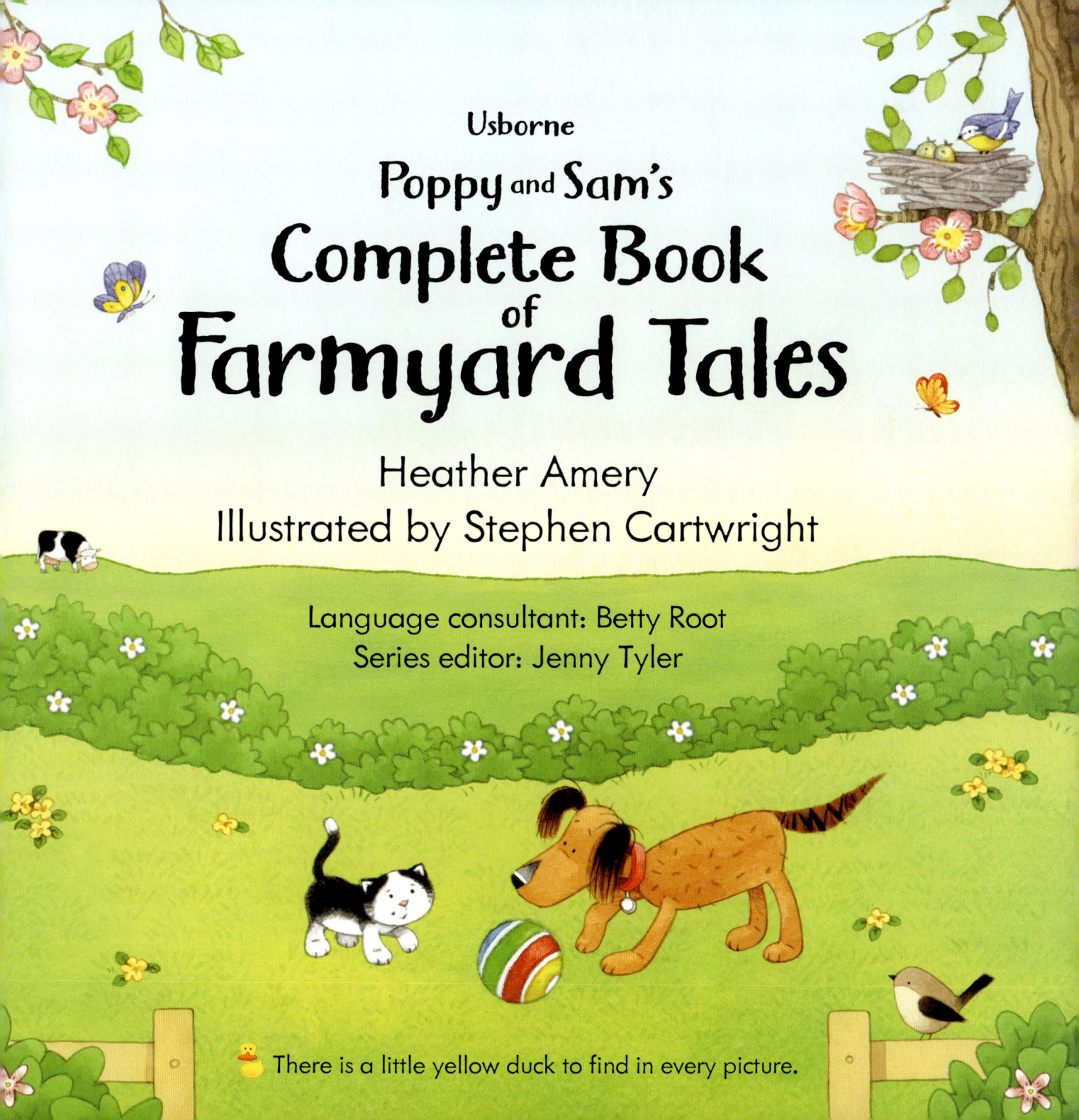

This book is dedicated
to the memory of
Stephen Cartwright

1948 - 2004

Contents

Pig Gets Stuck	1	The New Pony	161
The Naughty Sheep	17	The Grumpy Goat	177
Barn on Fire	33	The Snow Storm	193
The Runaway Tractor	49	Surprise Visitors	209
Pig Gets Lost	65	Market Day	225
The Hungry Donkey	81	Camping Out	241
Scarecrow's Secret	97	The Old Steam Train	257
Tractor in Trouble	113	Dolly and the Train	273
The Silly Sheepdog	129	Rusty's Train Ride	289
Kitten's Day Out	145	Woolly Stops the Train	305

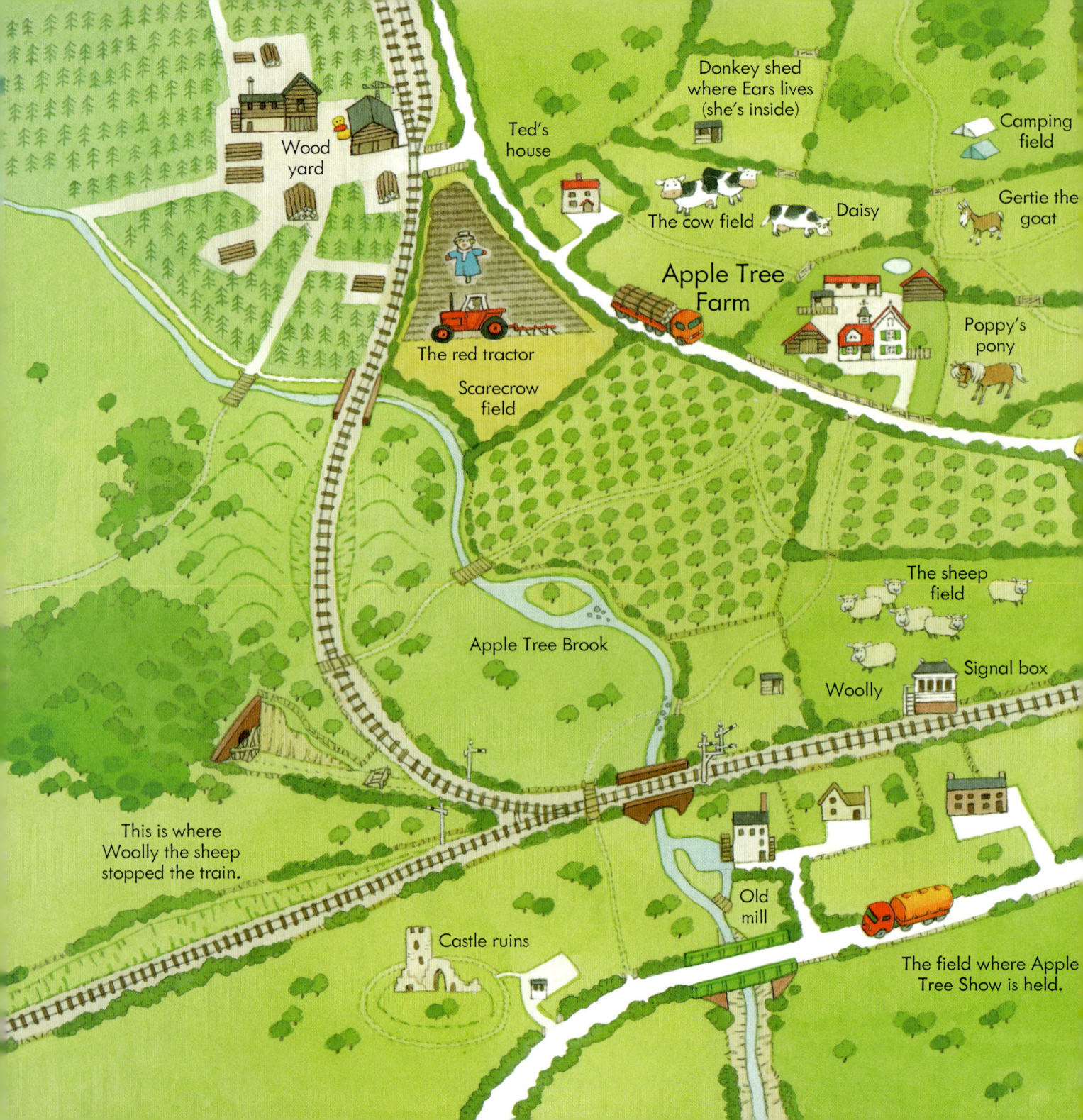

Pig Gets Stuck

This is Apple Tree Farm.

This is Mrs. Boot, the farmer. She has two children, called Poppy and Sam, and a dog called Rusty.

On the farm there are six pigs.

The pigs live in a pen with a little house.
The smallest pig is called Curly.

It is time for breakfast.

Mrs. Boot gives the pigs their breakfast.
But Curly is so small, he does not get any.

Curly is hungry.

He looks for something else to eat in the pen.
Then he finds a little gap under the wire.

Curly is out.

He squeezes through the gap under the wire.
He is out in the farmyard.

He meets lots of other animals in the farmyard.
Which breakfast would he like to eat?

Curly wants the hens' breakfast.

He thinks the hens' breakfast looks good.
He squeezes through the gap in the fence.

Curly tries it.

The hens' food is so good, he gobbles it all up.
The hens are not pleased.

Mrs. Boot sees Curly.

Curly hears Mrs. Boot shouting at him.
"What are you doing in the hen run, Curly?"

He runs to the fence.

He tries to squeeze through the gap. But he has eaten so much breakfast, he is too fat.

Curly is stuck.

Curly pushes and pushes but he can't move.
He is stuck in the fence.

They all push.

Mrs. Boot, Poppy and Sam all push Curly.
He squeals and squeals. His sides hurt.

Curly is out.

Then with a grunt, Curly pops through the fence.
"He's out, he's out!" shouts Sam.

He is safe now.

Mrs. Boot picks up Curly. "Poor little pig," she says. And she carries him back to the pig pen.

Curly is happy.

"Tomorrow you shall have lots of breakfast," she says. And Curly was never, ever hungry again.

The Naughty Sheep

This is Apple Tree Farm.

This is Mrs. Boot, the farmer. She has two children, called Poppy and Sam, and a dog called Rusty.

On the farm there are seven sheep.

The sheep live in a big field with a fence around it. One sheep has a black eye. She is called Woolly.

Woolly is bored.

Woolly stops eating and looks over the fence.
"Grass," she says. "Nothing but grass. Boring."

Woolly runs out of the gate.

She runs out of the field into the farmyard. Then she runs through another gate into a garden.

Woolly sees lots to eat in the garden.

She tastes some of the flowers. "Very good," she says, "and much prettier than grass."

Can you see where Woolly walked?

She walks around the garden, eating lots of the flowers. "I like flowers," she says.

Mrs. Boot sees Woolly in the garden.

"What are you doing in my garden?" she shouts. "You've eaten my flowers, you naughty sheep."

Mrs. Boot is very cross.

"It's the Show today," she says. "I was going to pick my best flowers for it. Just look at them."

It is time for the Show.

"Come on," says Poppy. "We must go now. The Show starts soon. It's only just down the road."

They all walk down the road.

Woolly watches them go. She chews her flower and thinks, "I'd like to go to the Show."

Woolly goes to the Show.

Woolly runs down the road. Soon she comes to a big field with lots of people in it.

Woolly goes into the ring.

She pushes past the people and into the field.
She stops by a man in a white coat.

Mrs. Boot finds her.

"What are you doing here, Woolly?" says Mrs. Boot.
"She has just won a prize," says the man.

Woolly is the winner.

"This cup is for the best sheep," says the man.
"Oh, that's lovely. Thank you," says Mrs. Boot.

It is time to go home.

"Come on, Woolly," says Mrs. Boot. "We'll take you back to your field, you naughty, clever sheep."

Barn on Fire

This is Apple Tree Farm.

This is Mrs. Boot, the farmer. She has two children, called Poppy and Sam, and a dog called Rusty.

This is Ted.

Ted works at Apple Tree Farm. He looks after the tractor and all the other farm machines.

Poppy and Sam help Ted.

They like helping Ted with jobs on the farm. Today he is fixing the fence around the sheep field.

Sam smells smoke.

"Ted," says Sam, "I think something's burning."
Ted stops working and they all sniff hard.

The barn is on fire.

"Look," says Poppy, "there's smoke coming from the hay barn. It must be on fire. What shall we do?"

"Call a fire engine."

"Come on," says Ted. "Run to the house. We must call a fire engine. Run as fast as you can."

Poppy and Sam run to the house.

"Help!" shouts Poppy. "Call a fire engine. Quickly! The hay barn is on fire."

Mrs. Boot dials the number.

"It's Apple Tree Farm," she says. "A fire engine please, as fast as you can. Thank you very much."

"You must stay here."

"Now, Poppy," says Mrs. Boot. "I want you and Sam to stay indoors. And don't let Rusty out."

Poppy and Sam watch from the door.

Soon they hear the siren. Then the fire engine roars up the road and into the farmyard.

"The firefighters are here."

The firefighters jump down from the engine.
They lift down lots of hoses and unroll them.

The firefighters run over to the barn with the hoses.
Can you see where they get the water from?

The firefighters squirt water onto the barn.

Poppy and Sam watch them from the window.
"It's still burning on the other side," says Poppy.

"There's the fire."

One firefighter runs behind the barn. What a surprise! Two campers are cooking on a big wood fire.

The fire is out.

"We're sorry," say the campers. "It was exciting," says Sam, "but I'm glad the barn is all right."

The Runaway Tractor

This is Apple Tree Farm.

This is Mrs. Boot, the farmer. She has two children, called Poppy and Sam, and a dog called Rusty.

Ted is the tractor driver.

He has filled the trailer with hay. He is taking it to the fields to feed the sheep.

Poppy and Sam hear a funny noise.

"Listen," says Poppy. "Ted is shouting and the tractor is making a funny noise. Let's go and look."

They run to the top of the hill.

The tractor is racing down the hill, going faster and faster. "It won't stop," shouts Ted.

The trailer comes off.

The trailer runs down the hill and crashes into a fence. It tips up and all the hay falls out.

The tractor runs into the pond.

The tractor hits the water with a great splash. The engine makes a loud noise, then it stops with a hiss.

Ted climbs down from the tractor.

Ted paddles through the water and out of the pond. Poppy and Sam run down the hill.

Ted is very wet.

Ted takes off his boots and tips out the water.
How can he get the tractor out of the pond?

"Go and ask Farmer Dray to help."

"Ask someone to telephone Farmer Dray," says Ted. Poppy and Sam run off to the house.

Farmer Dray has a big horse.

Soon he walks down the hill with his horse.
It is a huge carthorse, called Dolly.

Ted helps with the ropes.

Farmer Dray ties the ropes to the horse.
Ted ties the other ends to the tractor.

Dolly pulls and pulls.

Very slowly the tractor starts to move.
Ted pushes as hard as he can and Dolly pulls.

Ted falls over.

The tractor jerks forward and Ted falls in the water. Now he is wet and muddy all over.

The tractor is out of the pond.

"Better leave the tractor to dry," says Farmer Dray. "Then you can get the engine going again."

Poppy and Sam ride home.

Farmer Dray lifts them onto Dolly's back.
But Ted is so muddy, he has to walk.

Pig Gets Lost

This is Apple Tree Farm.

This is Mrs. Boot, the farmer. She has two children, called Poppy and Sam, and a dog called Rusty.

Mrs. Boot has six pigs.

There is a mother pig and five baby pigs.
The smallest pig is called Curly. They live in a pen.

Mrs. Boot feeds the pigs every morning.

She takes them two big buckets of food.
But where is Curly? He is not in the pen.

She calls Poppy and Sam.

"Curly's gone," she says.
"I need your help to find him."

"Where are you, Curly?"

Poppy and Sam call to Curly. "Let's look in the hen run," says Mrs. Boot. But Curly is not there.

"There he is, in the barn."

"He's in the barn," says Sam. "I can just see his tail." They all run into the barn to catch Curly.

"That's not Curly."

"It's only a piece of rope," says Mrs. Boot. "Not Curly's tail." "Where can he be?" says Poppy.

"Maybe he's eating the cows' food."

But Curly is not with the cows. "Don't worry," says Mrs. Boot. "We'll soon find him."

"Perhaps he's in the garden."

They look for Curly in the garden, but he is not there. "We'll never find him," says Sam.

"Why is Rusty barking?"

Rusty is standing by a ditch. He barks and barks.
"He's trying to tell us something," says Poppy.

"Rusty has found Curly."

They all look in the ditch. Curly has slipped down into the mud and can't climb out.

"We'll have to lift him out."

"I'll get into the ditch," says Mrs. Boot. "I'm coming too," says Poppy. "And me," says Sam.

Curly is very muddy.

Mrs. Boot picks Curly up but he struggles.
Then he slips back into the mud with a splash.

Now everyone is very muddy.

Sam tries to catch Curly but he falls into the mud.
Mrs. Boot grabs Curly and climbs out of the ditch.

They all climb out of the ditch.

"We all need a good bath," says Mrs. Boot.
"Rusty found Curly. Clever dog," says Sam.

The Hungry Donkey

This is Apple Tree Farm.

This is Mrs. Boot, the farmer. She has two children, called Poppy and Sam, and a dog called Rusty.

There is a donkey on the farm.

The donkey is called Ears. She lives in a field with lots of grass, but she is always hungry.

Ears the donkey is going out.

Poppy and Sam catch Ears and take her to the farmyard. Today is the day of the Show.

Ears has a little cart.

They brush her coat, comb her tail and clean her feet. Mrs. Boot puts her into her little cart.

Off they go to the Show.

Poppy and Sam climb up into the cart. They all go down the lane to the showground.

"You stay here, Ears."

At the showground, Mrs. Boot ties Ears to a fence. "Stay here. We'll be back soon," she says.

Ears gets free.

Ears is hungry and bored with nothing to do.
She pulls and pulls on the rope until she is free.

Ears looks for food.

Ears trots across the field to the show ring.
She sees a bunch of flowers and some fruit.

"That looks good to eat."

She takes a big bite, but the flowers do not taste very nice. A lady screams and Ears is frightened.

Ears runs away.

Mrs. Boot, Poppy and Sam and the lady run after her and catch her.

"Naughty donkey," says Sam.

"I'm sorry," Mrs. Boot says to the lady. "Would you like to take Ears to the best donkey competition?"

Ears is very good now.

The lady is called Mrs. Rose. She climbs into the cart. "Come on," she says, and shakes the reins.

Ears pulls the cart into the show ring.

She trots in front of the judges. She stops and goes when Mrs. Rose tells her.

Ears wins a prize.

"Well done," says the judge, giving her a rosette.
He gives Mrs. Rose a prize too. It is a hat.

It is time to go home.

Mrs. Rose waves goodbye. "That was such fun," she says. Ears trots home. She has a new hat too.

Scarecrow's Secret

This is Apple Tree Farm.

This is Mrs. Boot, the farmer. She has two children, called Poppy and Sam, and a dog called Rusty.

Mr. Boot is working in the barn.

"What are you doing, Dad?" asks Sam. "I'm tying lots of straw on these poles," says Mr. Boot.

"What is it?"

"You'll soon see," says Mr. Boot. "Go and get my old coat from the shed, please. Bring my old hat too."

"It's going to be a scarecrow."

Poppy and Sam come back with the coat and hat. Then they help Mr. Boot put them on the scarecrow.

"He's just like a nice old man."

"I've got some old gloves for him," says Sam.
"Let's call him Mr. Straw," says Poppy.

"He's finished now."

"Help me carry him, please, Poppy," says Mr. Boot. "You bring the shovel, Sam."

They all go to the cornfield.

Mr. Boot digs a hole in the field. Then he pushes in the pole so that Mr. Straw stands up.

"He does look real."

"I'm sure Mr. Straw will scare off all the birds," says Sam. "Especially the crows," says Poppy.

Mr. Straw is doing a good job.

Every day, Mr. Boot, Poppy and Sam look at Mr. Straw. There are no birds in the cornfield.

"There's Farmer Dray's scarecrow."

"He's no good at all," says Sam. "The birds are eating all the corn and standing on the scarecrow."

"Why is Mr. Straw so good?"

"Sometimes he looks as if he is moving," says Poppy. "His coat goes up and down. It's very odd."

"Let's go and look."

"Let's creep up very quietly," says Sam. And they tiptoe across the cornfield to look at Mr. Straw.

"There's something inside his coat."

"It's moving," says Poppy. "And it's making a funny noise. What is it?" says Sam.

"It's our cat and her kittens."

Carefully they open the coat. There is Whiskers, the cat, and two baby kittens hiding in the straw.

"So that's the scarecrow's secret."

"Whiskers is helping Mr. Straw to frighten off the birds," says Poppy. "Clever Mr. Straw," says Sam.

Tractor in Trouble

This is Apple Tree Farm.

This is Mrs. Boot, the farmer. She has two children, called Poppy and Sam, and a dog called Rusty.

Ted works on the farm.

He helps Mrs. Boot. Ted looks after the tractor and all the farm machines.

Today it is very windy.

The wind is blowing the trees and it is very cold. Poppy and Sam play in the barn.

"Where are you going, Ted?"

Ted is driving the tractor out of the yard. "I'm just going to see if the sheep are all right," he says.

Ted stops the tractor by the gate.

He goes into the sheep field. He nails down the roof of the sheep shed to make it safe.

Poppy and Sam hear a terrible crash.

"What's that?" says Sam. "I don't know. Let's go and look," says Poppy. They run down the field.

"A tree has blown down."

"It's come down on Ted's tractor," says Poppy.
"Come on. We must help him," says Sam.

"What are you going to do, Ted?"

Poor Ted is very upset. The tree has scratched his new tractor. He can't even get into the cab.

"Ask Farmer Dray to help."

"I think I can see him on the hill," says Ted.
Poppy and Sam run to ask him.

Soon Farmer Dray comes with his horse.

Farmer Dray has a big, gentle carthorse, called Dolly. They have come to help Ted.

"I'll cut up the tree first."

Farmer Dray starts up his chainsaw. Then he cuts off the branches which have fallen on the tractor.

Dolly starts to work.

Farmer Dray ties two ropes to Dolly's harness.
Ted ties the other ends to the big branches.

Dolly pulls and pulls.

She works hard until all the branches are off the tractor. "Well done, Dolly," says Farmer Dray.

Ted climbs up into the cab.

"Thank you very much, Farmer Dray and Dolly," he says. And they all go back to the farmyard.

The tractor looks a little messy.

Ted finds a brush and paints over all the scratches.
"It will soon be as good as new," he says.

The Silly Sheepdog

This is Apple Tree Farm.

This is Mrs. Boot, the farmer. She has two children, called Poppy and Sam, and a dog called Rusty.

Ted works on Apple Tree Farm.

He has just bought a sheepdog to help him with the sheep. The sheepdog is called Patch.

Poppy, Sam and Rusty say hello to Patch.

"Come on, Patch," says Sam. "We'll show you all the animals on our farm."

First they look at the hens.

Patch jumps into the hen run and chases the hens.
They are frightened and fly up onto their house.

"Now we'll go and see the cows."

Patch runs into the field and barks at the cows.
But they just stand and stare at him.

Then they look at the pigs.

Patch jumps into the pig pen and chases all the pigs into their little house.

Sam shouts at Patch.

"Come here, you silly thing. You're meant to be a sheepdog. Ted will have to send you back."

They go to the sheep field.

"Look," says Sam. "One sheep is missing."
"Yes, it's that naughty Woolly again," says Ted.

"Where's Patch going?" says Sam.

Patch runs away across the field. Ted, Sam, Poppy and Rusty run after him.

Patch dives through the hedge.

Patch barks and barks. "What has he found?" says Sam. They all go to look.

Patch has found a boy.

The boy pats Patch. "Hello," he says. "I wondered who bought you when my dad sold his farm."

The boy has found a sheep.

"There's Woolly," says Sam. "I found her on the road," says the boy. "I was bringing her back."

The boy whistles to Patch.

Patch chases Woolly back through the gate.
She runs into the field with the other sheep.

Ted stares in surprise.

"Patch doesn't do anything I tell him," says Ted.
"You don't know how to whistle," says the boy.

Patch runs back to them.

"You must teach me how to whistle to Patch," says Ted. "He's not a silly dog after all," says Sam.

Kitten's Day Out

This is Apple Tree Farm.

This is Mrs. Boot, the farmer. She has two children, called Poppy and Sam, and a dog called Rusty.

Ted works on the farm.

He is helping Mr. Bran, the truck driver. Mr. Bran has brought some sacks of food for the cows.

They say goodbye to Mr. Bran.

Mr. Bran waves as he drives his truck out of the farmyard. Ted and Poppy wave back.

"Where's my kitten?"

"Where's Fluff?" says Sam. They all look everywhere for Fluff. But they can't find her.

"Perhaps she jumped on the truck."

"Take my car and go after the truck, Ted," says Mrs. Boot. They jump in the car and drive off.

Ted stops the car at the crossroads.

"Which way did Mr. Bran go?" says Ted. "There's a truck," says Sam. "It's just going around the bend."

Ted drives down a steep hill.

"Look out, Ted," says Poppy. There's a stream at the bottom. The car splashes into the water.

The car stops in the stream.

"Water in the engine," says Ted. "I'll have to push."
"We'll never find the truck now," says Sam.

Ted looks inside the car.

He mops up all the water. Soon he gets the car to start again. They drive on to look for the truck.

There are lots of sheep on the road.

"The sheep came out of the field. Someone left the gate open," says Ted. "We must get them back."

Ted, Poppy and Sam round up the sheep.

They drive them back into the field. Ted shuts the gate. "Come on, we must hurry," says Sam.

"Stop, Ted, there's a truck."

"I'm sure that's Mr. Bran's truck in that farmyard," says Sam. Ted drives in to see.

"It's the wrong truck."

"Oh dear," says Poppy. "It's not Mr. Bran, and that's not Mr. Bran's truck."

Ted drives them home.

"We'll never find my kitten now," says Sam.
"I'm sure she'll turn up," says Poppy.

There's a surprise at Apple Tree Farm.

"Here's your kitten," says Mr. Bran. "She's been in my truck all day and now I've brought her home."

The New Pony

This is Apple Tree Farm.

This is Mrs. Boot, the farmer. She has two children, called Poppy and Sam, and a dog called Rusty.

Mr. Boot, Poppy and Sam go for a walk.

They see a new pony. "She belongs to Mr. Stone, who's just bought Old Gate Farm," says Mr. Boot.

The pony looks sad.

Her coat is rough and dirty. She looks hungry.
It looks as though no one takes care of her.

Poppy tries to stroke the pony.

"She's not very friendly," says Sam. "Mr. Stone says she's bad tempered," says Mr. Boot.

Poppy feeds the pony.

Every day, Poppy takes her apples and carrots.
But she always stays on the other side of the gate.

One day, Poppy takes Sam with her.

They cannot see the pony anywhere. The field looks empty. "Where is she?" says Sam.

Poppy and Sam open the gate.

Rusty runs into the field. Poppy and Sam are a bit scared. "We must find the pony," says Poppy.

"There she is," says Sam.

The pony has caught her head collar in the fence.
She has been eating the grass on the other side.

Poppy and Sam run home to Mr. Boot.

"Please come and help us, Dad," says Poppy. "The pony is caught in the fence. She will hurt herself."

Mr. Boot walks up to the pony.

He unhooks the pony's head collar from the fence. "She's not hurt," says Mr. Boot.

"The pony's chasing us."

"Quick, run," says Sam. "It's all right," says Poppy, patting the pony. "She just wants to be friends."

They see an angry man. It is Mr. Stone.

"Leave my pony alone," says Mr. Stone. "And get out of my field." He shakes his fist at Poppy.

The pony is afraid of Mr. Stone.

Mr. Stone waves his arms angrily at the pony.
"I'm going to get rid of that nasty animal," he says.

Poppy grabs his arm.

"You mustn't scare the pony," she cries. "Come on, Poppy," says Mr. Boot. "Let's go home."

Next day, there's a surprise for Poppy.

The pony is at Apple Tree Farm. "We've bought her for you," says Mrs. Boot. "Thank you," says Poppy.

The Grumpy Goat

This is Apple Tree Farm.

This is Mrs. Boot, the farmer. She has two children, called Poppy and Sam, and a dog called Rusty.

Ted works on the farm.

He tells Poppy and Sam to clean the goat's shed.
"Will she let us?" asks Sam. "She's so grumpy now."

Gertie the goat chases Sam.

She butts him with her head. He nearly falls over. Sam, Poppy and Rusty run out through the gate.

Poppy shuts the gate.

They must get Gertie out of her pen so they can get to her shed. "I have an idea," says Sam.

Sam gets a bag of bread.

"Come on, Gertie," says Sam. "Nice bread."
Gertie eats it and the bag, but stays in her pen.

"Let's try some fresh grass," says Poppy.

Poppy pulls up some grass and drops it by the gate.
Gertie eats it but trots back into her pen.

"I have another idea," says Sam.

"Gertie doesn't butt Ted. She wouldn't butt me if I looked like Ted," says Sam. He runs off again.

Sam comes back wearing Ted's clothes.

He has found Ted's old coat and hat. Sam goes into the pen but Gertie still butts him.

"I'll get a rope," says Poppy.

They go into the pen. Poppy tries to throw the rope over Gertie's head. She misses.

Gertie chases them all.

Rusty runs out of the pen and Gertie follows him.
"She's out!" shouts Sam. "Quick, shut the gate."

Sam and Poppy clean out Gertie's shed.

They sweep up the old straw and put it in the wheelbarrow. They spread out fresh straw.

Poppy opens the gate.

"Come on, Gertie. You can go back now," says Sam. Gertie trots back into her pen.

"You are a grumpy old goat," says Poppy.

"We've cleaned out your shed and you're still grumpy," says Sam. "Grumpy Gertie."

Next morning, they meet Ted.

"Come and look at Gertie now," says Ted.
They all go to the goat pen.

Gertie has a little kid.

"Oh, isn't it sweet," says Poppy. "Gertie doesn't look grumpy now," says Sam.

The Snow Storm

This is Apple Tree Farm.

This is Mrs. Boot, the farmer. She has two children, called Poppy and Sam, and a dog called Rusty.

In the night there was a big snow storm.

In the morning, it is still snowing. "You must wrap up warm," says Mrs. Boot to Poppy and Sam.

Ted works on the farm.

He helps Mrs. Boot look after the animals.
He gives them food and water every day.

"Come and help me," calls Ted.

"Where are you going?" says Poppy. "I'm taking this hay to the sheep," says Ted.

Poppy and Sam pull the hay.

They go out of the farmyard with Ted.
They walk to the gate of the sheep field.

"Where are the sheep?" says Sam.

"They are all covered with snow," says Ted.
"We'll have to find them," says Poppy.

They brush the snow off the sheep.

Ted, Poppy and Sam give each sheep lots of hay.
"They've got nice warm coats," says Sam.

Poppy counts the sheep.

"There are only six sheep. One is missing," says Poppy. "It's that naughty Woolly," says Ted.

They look for Woolly.

They walk around the snowy field.
"Rusty, good dog, find Woolly," calls Sam.

Rusty runs across the field.

Ted, Poppy and Sam run after him.
Rusty barks at the thick hedge.

Ted looks under the hedge.

"Can you see anything?" says Sam. "Yes, Woolly is hiding in there. Clever Rusty," says Ted.

"Come on, Woolly."

"Let me help you out, old girl," says Ted.
Carefully he pulls Woolly out of the hedge.

"There's something else!"

"Look, I can see something moving," says Sam.
"What is it, Ted?" says Poppy.

Ted lifts out a tiny lamb.

"Woolly has had a lamb," he says. "We'll take it and Woolly to the barn. They'll be warm there."

Poppy rides home.

She holds the lamb. "What a surprise!" she says. "Good old Woolly."

Surprise Visitors

This is Apple Tree Farm.

This is Mrs. Boot, the farmer. She has two children, called Poppy and Sam, and a dog called Rusty.

Today is Saturday.

Mrs. Boot, Poppy and Sam are having breakfast.
"Why are the cows so noisy?" asks Sam.

They all run out to the field.

The cows are running around the field. They are scared. A big balloon is floating over the trees.

"It's a hot-air balloon."

"It's coming down," says Mrs. Boot. "It's going to land in our field." The balloon hits the ground.

There are two people in it.

"Where are we?" asks the man. "This is Apple Tree Farm. You frightened our cows," says Mrs. Boot.

The man climbs out.

"I'm Alice and this is Tim," says the woman. "We ran out of gas. Sorry about your cows."

"A truck is following us."

"There it is now," says Alice. "Our friend is bringing more cylinders of gas for the balloon."

Alice helps to unload the truck.

Tim unloads the empty cylinders. Then he puts the new ones into the balloon's basket.

They blow up the balloon.

Poppy and Sam help Tim hold open the balloon.
A fan blows hot air into it. It gets bigger and bigger.

"Would you like a ride?"

"Oh, yes please," says Poppy. "Just a little one," says Tim. "The truck will bring you back."

Mrs. Boot, Poppy and Sam climb in.

Tim lights the gas burner. The big flames make a loud noise. "Hold on tight," says Alice.

The balloon goes up.

Slowly it leaves the ground. Tim turns off the burner. "The wind is blowing us along," he says.

The balloon floats along.

"I can see our farm down there," says Poppy.
"Look, there's Alice in the truck," says Sam.

"We're going down now," says Tim.

The balloon floats down and the basket lands in a field. Mrs. Boot helps Poppy and Sam out.

"Thank you very much."

They wave as the balloon takes off again.
"We were flying," says Sam.

Market Day

This is Apple Tree Farm.

This is Mrs. Boot, the farmer. She has two children, called Poppy and Sam, and a dog called Rusty.

Today is market day.

Mrs. Boot puts the trailer on the car. Poppy and Sam put a wire crate in the trailer.

They drive to the market.

Mrs. Boot, Poppy and Sam walk past cows, sheep and pigs. They go to the shed that has cages of birds.

There are different kinds of geese.

"Let's look in all the cages," says Mrs. Boot. "I want four nice young geese."

"There are four nice white ones."

"They look nice and friendly," says Poppy.
"Yes, they are just what I want," says Mrs. Boot.

A woman is selling the geese.

"How much are the four white ones?" asks Mrs. Boot. "I'll buy them, please." She pays for them.

"We'll come back later."

"Let's look at the other birds," says Sam. There are cages with hens, chicks, ducks and pigeons.

"Look at the poor little duck."

"It's lonely," says Poppy. "Please may I buy it? I can pay for it with my own money."

"Yes, you can buy it."

"We'll get it when we come back for the geese," says Mrs. Boot. Poppy pays the man for the duck.

Mrs. Boot brings the crate.

Poppy opens the lid. The woman passes the geese to Mrs. Boot. She puts them in the crate.

One of the geese runs away.

A goose jumps out of the crate just before Sam shuts the lid. It runs very fast out of the shed.

"Catch that goose!"

Mrs. Boot, Poppy and Sam run after the goose.
The goose jumps through an open car door.

"Now we've got it," says Sam.

But a woman opens a door on the other side.
The goose jumps out of the car and runs away.

"Run after it," says Mrs. Boot.

The goose runs into the plant tent.
"There it is," says Sam, and picks it up.

"Let's go home," says Mrs. Boot.

"I've got my geese now." "And I've got my duck," says Poppy. "Markets are fun," says Sam.

Camping Out

This is Apple Tree Farm.

This is Mrs. Boot, the farmer. She has two children, called Poppy and Sam, and a dog called Rusty.

A car stops at the gate.

A man, a woman and a boy get out.
"Hello," says the man. "May we camp on your farm?"

"Yes, you can camp over there."

"We'll show you the way," says Mr. Boot.
The campers follow in the car.

The campers put up their tent.

Poppy and Sam help them. They take chairs, a table, a cooking stove and food out of the car.

Then they all go to the farmhouse.

Mrs. Boot gives the campers a bucket of water and some milk. Poppy and Sam bring some eggs.

"Can we go camping?"

"Please, Dad, can we put up our tent too?" says Poppy. "Oh yes, please, Dad," says Sam.

Mrs. Boot gets out the tent.

Poppy and Sam try to put up the little blue tent, but it keeps falling down. At last it is ready.

"Come and have supper."

"Then you can go to the tent," says Mrs. Boot. "But you must wash and brush your teeth first."

Poppy and Sam go to the tent.

"It's not dark yet," says Sam. "Come on, Rusty. You can come camping with us," says Poppy.

Poppy and Sam go to bed.

They crawl into the tent and tie up the door.
Then they wriggle into their sleeping bags.

"What's that noise?"

Sam sits up. "There's something walking around outside the tent," says Sam. "What is it?"

Poppy looks out of the tent.

"It's only Daisy, the cow," she says. "She must have strayed into this field. She's so nosy."

Daisy looks into the tent.

Rusty barks at her. Daisy is scared. She tries to back away but the tent catches on her head.

Daisy pulls at the tent.

She pulls it down and runs off with it. Rusty chases her. Poppy and Sam run back to the house.

Mr. Boot opens the door.

"Hello, Dad," says Sam. "Daisy's got our tent."
"I think camping is fun," says Poppy.

The Old Steam Train

This is Apple Tree Farm.

This is Mrs. Boot, the farmer. She has two children, called Poppy and Sam, and a dog called Rusty.

"Hurry up," says Mrs. Boot.

"Where are we going today?" asks Poppy.
"To the old station," says Mrs. Boot.

They walk down the lane.

"Why are we going? There aren't any trains," says Sam. "Just you wait and see," says Mrs. Boot.

"What's everyone doing?" asks Poppy.

"They're cleaning up the old station," says Mrs. Boot. "Everyone's helping today."

"There's lots to do."

"Poppy and Sam can help me," says the painter.
"Coats off and down to work," says Mrs. Boot.

Poppy and Sam work hard.

Sam brings pots of paint and Poppy brings the brushes. Mrs. Boot sweeps the platform.

"What's that noise?"

"It's the train. It's coming," says Mrs. Boot. "Look, it's a steam train," says Poppy. "How exciting."

The train puffs down the track.

It stops at the platform. The engine gives a long whistle. Everyone cheers and waves.

"Look, there's Dad," says Sam.

"He's helping the driver, just for today," says Mrs. Boot. "Isn't he lucky?" says Poppy.

"All aboard," says Mrs. Boot.

"I'll get on here," says Poppy. "Come on, Rusty," says Sam. "I'll shut the door," says Mrs. Boot.

"Where are you going?"

"Aren't you coming with us?" asks Sam. "You stay on the train," says Mrs. Boot. "I'll be back soon."

"Look, there she is."

"She's wearing a cap," says Poppy. "Yes, I'm the guard, just for today," says Mrs. Boot.

Mrs. Boot waves a flag.

The train whistles and starts to puff away.
Mrs. Boot jumps on the train and shuts the door.

"We're off," says Sam.

The train chugs slowly down the track. "Doesn't the old station look good now?" says Poppy.

"I like steam trains," says Sam.

"The station is open again," says Mrs. Boot. "And we can ride on the steam train every weekend."

Dolly and the Train

This is Apple Tree Farm.

This is Mrs. Boot, the farmer. She has two children, called Poppy and Sam, and a dog called Rusty.

Today there is a school outing.

Mrs. Boot, Poppy and Sam walk down the road to the old station. "Come on, Rusty," says Sam.

"There's your teacher," says Mrs. Boot.

"And there's the old steam train, all ready for our outing," says Poppy.

"All aboard," says the driver.

The children and their teacher climb on the train.
The guard closes the door and blows his whistle.

Mrs. Boot waves goodbye.

The train puffs slowly down the track. Rusty barks at it. He wants to go on the outing too.

The children look out of the window.

"I can see Farmer Dray's farm," says Sam.
"Why has the train stopped?" asks Poppy.

"The engine has broken down."

"We'll have to send for help," says the driver. "It won't be long." The guard runs across the fields.

"Here's a ladder."

"You can all get off now," says the driver.
"We can have our picnic here," says the teacher.

"Let's go into the field," says Sam.

The children climb over the fence. "Stop! Come back, children," says the teacher. "There's a bull."

"It's only Buttercup."

"She's not a bull. She's a very nice cow," says Poppy.
"Well, come back here," says the teacher.

"Look, there's Farmer Dray."

"He's brought Dolly with him," says Sam. "A horse is no good. We need an engine," says the teacher.

The children watch.

Farmer Dray has a long rope. He leads Dolly along the train. The driver unhitches the engine.

The children climb back on the train.

"We'll soon be off now," says the teacher.
"Dolly's ready," says Farmer Dray.

"Pull away, Dolly."

Dolly pulls and pulls. Very slowly the train starts to move. Farmer Dray walks along with Dolly.

They reach the station.

"Out by engine, back by horse," says Farmer Dray.
"That was a good outing," says Sam.

Rusty's Train Ride

This is Apple Tree Farm.

This is Mrs. Boot, the farmer. She has two children, called Poppy and Sam, and a dog called Rusty.

They are having breakfast.

"What are we doing today?" says Sam. "Let's go and see the old steam train," says Mrs. Boot.

"Come on, Rusty," says Sam.

They walk down the road to the station. "Don't let Rusty go. Hold him tight," says Mrs. Boot.

They wait on the platform.

Mrs. Boot, Poppy and Sam watch the train come in.
Mrs. Hill and her puppy watch with them.

The train is ready to go.

Everyone talks to the train driver. The fireman shuts the doors. He climbs on the train.

"Where's my puppy?"

"Mopp was with me on the platform," says Mrs. Hill. "Now he's gone." The train starts to move.

Rusty watches it go.

He pulls and pulls and runs away. Then he jumps through an open carriage window.

"Come back, Rusty," shouts Sam.

Rusty looks out of the window. "There he is," says Poppy. "He's going for a train ride on his own."

"Stop! Stop the train," shouts Sam.

Mrs. Boot, Poppy and Sam shout and wave.
But the train puffs away down the track.

"What shall we do?"

"Both dogs have gone," says Sam. "We'll have to wait for the train to come back," says Mrs. Boot.

At last, the train comes back.

"Look, there's Rusty," says Sam. "You naughty dog, where have you been?" says Poppy.

The train stops at the station.

The fireman climbs down from the engine.
He opens the carriage door.

"Come on, Rusty."

"Your ride on the train is over," says Mrs. Boot. Rusty jumps down. "What's he got?" says Sam.

"It's my little Mopp."

Mrs. Hill picks up her puppy. "Poor little thing. Did you go on the train all by yourself?"

"Rusty went with him," says Sam.

"That's why he jumped on the train," says Poppy.
"Clever Rusty," says Sam.

Woolly Stops the Train

This is Apple Tree Farm.

This is Mrs. Boot, the farmer. She has two children, called Poppy and Sam, and a dog called Rusty.

This is Ted.

He drives the tractor and helps Mrs. Boot on the farm. He waves and shouts to Mrs. Boot.

"What's the matter, Ted?" asks Mrs. Boot.

"The train is in trouble. I think it's stuck. I can hear it whistling and whistling," says Ted.

"We'll go and look."

"Poppy and Sam can come too," says Mrs. Boot.
"And Rusty," says Sam. They walk across the fields.

Soon they come to the train track.

They can just see the old steam train. It has stopped but is still puffing and whistling.

"Look at those sheep."

"They are on the track," says Poppy. "That's why the train has stopped." "Silly sheep," says Sam.

"It's that naughty Woolly."

"She's escaped from her field again," says Poppy.
"She wanted to see the steam train," says Sam.

"I will move them."

"All of you stay there," says Ted. "You must never walk on the track. It's not safe."

The sheep won't move.

Woolly and the other naughty sheep are still on the track. They will not go up the bank.

"Come on, sheep."

Ted has an idea. He herds the sheep down the track. "I'll have to put you on the train," he says.

"I will help you."

The train driver helps Ted lift the sheep up into the carriage. "Thank you, driver," says Ted.

"All aboard!"

"I've never had sheep on my train before!" says the driver. The train puffs away.

"Here's the train!"

Poppy, Sam and Mrs. Boot are waiting on the platform. The train stops. Mrs. Boot opens the door.

"How many passengers?" says the guard.

"Six sheep and one person," says Ted. "That's all."
"Well done, Ted!" say Poppy and Sam.

"Let's all go home now," says Mrs. Boot.

They take the sheep back to the farm. "I think Woolly just wanted a ride on the train," says Sam.